THIS BOOK BELONGS TO:

....

J K

I am a reader and I celebrated
World Book Day 2024 with this book
from a local bookseller and Farshore.

*To all the brilliant young people I've met on my author travels.
I hope you have as much fun reading this as I did writing it.*

First published in Great Britain in 2024 by Farshore
An imprint of HarperCollins*Publishers*
1 London Bridge Street, London SE1 9GF

farshore.co.uk

HarperCollins*Publishers*
Macken House, 39/40 Mayor Street Upper, Dublin 1, D01 C9W8

Text copyright © Jennifer Killick 2024

The moral rights of the author and illustrator have been asserted

ISBN 978-0-00-865207-4

Printed and bound in the UK using 100% renewable electricity at
CPI Group (UK) Ltd

1

A CIP catalogue record for this title is available from the British Library.

This book contains FSC™ certified paper and other controlled
sources to ensure responsible forest management.

For more information visit: www.harpercollins.co.uk/green

World Book Day® and the associated logo are the registered trademarks of World Book Day® Limited.
Registered charity number 1079257 (England and Wales). Registered company number 03783095 (

DREAD WOOD
CREEPY CREATIONS

World Book Day's mission is to offer every child and young person the opportunity to read and love books by giving you the chance to have a book of your own.

To find out more, and for fun activities including video stories, audiobooks and book recommendations, visit worldbookday.com

World Book Day is a charity sponsored by National Book Tokens.

CHAPTER ONE

CLUB LOSER

'**W**elcome to Dread Wood High. If you've ever wanted to be chased around the grounds by evil maniacs in clown masks while parasitic worms chew on your brain, then this is the school for you.' I grin and turn to Mr Canton, our teacher, who is busy ticking things off a piece of paper attached to his trusty clipboard. 'How was that?'

'Not sure that's the impression we want to give, Angelo,' Mr C says from deep in his list.

Me, Colette, Hallie, Gus and Naira are sitting in student services – a huge room with comfy sofas and quiet corners – drinking hot chocolate from the vending machine. It's the best place in school besides the well-being pig yard and the silent trees in the Dread Wood, where I always feel happy, even with all the things that have happened there.

My friends and I have found ourselves in student services A LOT over the past year, being summoned for check-ins after the traumas and dramas of school life. And traumas and dramas at Dread Wood High are on another level from failing exams or getting caught scratching graffiti on the desks . . . this is a school like no other, or at least it has been for us, Club Loser.

Mr C rushes around us, getting the room ready for a load of Year 5 kids and their parents who are coming to suss out Dread Wood High.

'Wait, you forgot about fist-fighting with genetically mutated giant spiders,' Hallie says, miming a fierce uppercut.

'Spiders don't have fists.' Naira raises an eyebrow. 'It was more like kick fighting. With added pointy sticks.'

Gus puts his hot chocolate down on the table and grabs a school prospectus from what was a neat pile. 'Yes, Nai-Nai! And I especially love that this could work in song form. Dread Wood High GOATED freestyle rap coming up . . . I'm gonna work on some lyrics.' He grabs one of Mr C's spare pens from his pocket and starts scribbling.

'As much as I hate to stifle your creativity,' Mr C looks up from his clipboard, 'now is not the time. We have T-minus ninety minutes until prospective students and their guardians arrive for Choccie Chat . . .'

We all roll our eyes, but smile too, because as much as Mr Canton is painful levels of cringe, we would never change him. And we definitely wouldn't want to calm his excitement for chatting with hot chocolate, because it's got us out of many dull minutes of biology and RE.

'If you write it down, then technically you can't call it freestyle.' Naira leans over Gus to see what he's writing. 'And that's not how you spell "decapitation".'

Gus ignores her and carries on.

'Let's not have any decapitation talk while there are visitors in the school . . .' Mr Canton is starting to look stressed. 'The focus should be on your positive experiences here: the wonderful facilities, the array of extra-curricular opportunities, the life-changing lessons . . .'

'Biggest lesson we've learned here is how to survive,' Hallie snorts.

'Dread Wood High – fight or die,' I say. 'That should be the new school motto.'

'OMG, writing that down too.' Gus is scrawling on the shiny DWH prospectus in a chaotic scribble and inserting sketches like he's Leonardo da Vinci having a moment of perfect inspiration. 'What even *is* the school motto?'

Hallie bum-shuffles across the sofa to read Gus's rap masterpiece. 'I didn't know we had one.'

Naira stares at Hallie like she's just said the stupidest thing ever. 'It's on the school crest.'

Hallie shrugs.

'The crest that's displayed in a hundred places around the school buildings?' Naira sighs. 'The crest that you are literally wearing on your blazer.'

We all look down at the embroidered badges on our uniforms like we've never noticed them before.

'Oh yeah!' Colette says. 'I always wondered what that said.'

'Fac fortia et patere,' Mr Canton says. 'And honestly, I can't believe you've been here for a whole year and have managed not to know about it.'

We all snigger, 'cos the start of it sounds like a swear. And Mr C is not the swearing type.

'I know you're stressed, sir, but there's no need for the language,' Colette says.

'It means "do brave deeds and endure".' Mr Canton's face has gone pinker than his tie. 'Actually not a million miles away from "fight or die".'

'You're kidding?' I say. 'Are they actually taking the mick?'

'They might as well advertise it as the school where nightmares turn real.' Colette shakes her head and we all look at each other for a moment.

'Wait, I need to get this right.' Gus looks up, pen ready to write. 'Can you repeat it for us, sir?'

'Of course.' Mr C nods. 'Fac fortia . . .'

~~We all crack up laughing.~~

'It means do!' Mr C says. 'DO!'

'You sound like a proper rapper, sir,' Gus says, still writing. 'This is all gold.'

Mr C sighs and puts his clipboard down on the table. 'Well, as you're insisting on ignoring my polite requests to take this evening seriously, I'm going to have to lean into this situation and join the band. Whattup, homies – shall I lay down some sick beats?'

'No!' we all shout. Mr C tries painfully hard to talk like a teenager, and it's so cringe that at times it makes us want to be dragged underground by human-eating spiders.

He starts beat-boxing and doing a hand movement that I think is supposed to be like he's scratching vinyl but looks more like his body is malfunctioning.

There are maybe three seconds of horrified silence from everyone else in the room, and then Gus puts the pen down on the table and holds his hands up. 'We agree to any and all demands.'

'Just. Please. Stop,' Hallie says.

'Right now.' Colette picks the pen off the table and puts it back in Mr C's pocket.

He grins and picks his clipboard up again.

At the start of Year 7 at Dread Wood High, none of

us were friends. I was angry and bored. Couldn't see the point of school when all I wanted to be doing was helping my family, earning money so we could pay rent, eat, keep the electric on for TV and gaming purposes – stuff like that. I put myself in this moody troublemaker box and decided I was better off alone. But then I was put in a Saturday detention with Hallie, Gus and Naira, and it changed everything. We had to work together to stay alive and to figure out why we were being targeted. I got to know them, respect them, and even trust them. And now I can't imagine going back to the angry loner I was before.

Mr C clears his throat and puts his serious face on. 'Now you know I have immense respect for all of you and what you've been through in the past year. You've shown more integrity and courage than anyone I've ever known, and I would never want to seem as though I am belittling your experiences or accomplishments . . .'

'But . . .' Hallie sighs.

'But . . .' Mr Canton puts his hand on her shoulder and Hallie rolls her eyes, 'this evening is a wholesome family event, and you five have been selected to represent the school because you're the best of Dread Wood High.'

'We're not though, are we?' Gus says. 'I mean, maybe Naira is. 'Cos yeah, she's A-star smart, and perfect if you turn a blind eye to her drunken nana at the karaoke singing and her embarrassing hair fails. But the rest of us . . . Why would Mr Hume – the sussiest head in the multiverse – choose us?' He looks around the group. 'No offence.'

'None taken,' I say. Because I've been in more than my share of trouble since I started here. 'I'm the last person I'd choose, except for maybe Hal.'

'Why me?' Hallie glares at me like I just stomped on her pet chicken. Hallie fights for what she believes in: equality, freedom and animal rights. She rescued her chicken, Michelle, from a spider-shaped death and loves her like a sister.

'Because you always fight on the side of truth and justice, no matter what it costs, like a shorter, rainbow-flag-holding Batman.' I shrug. 'Also, you've got the raging unpredictability of an angry cat.'

'Ah, thanks, Angelo! That's actually lovely.' Hallie smiles at me.

'I would've picked Col, though,' I say.

Gus pretends to vom, and throws a cushion at me, which I'm ready for and expertly catch with a grin.

'Aw, relationship goals,' Hallie says.

'Excuse me, I'm totally pickable,' Colette says. 'Like, I get good grades, I got subject star for art last year *and . . .'* her face breaks into an evil grin, 'unlike the rest of you, I've never had a detention.'

Four cushions fly her way as the rest of us luz them at her with varying levels of accuracy. Me, Hallie, Gus and Naira getting that Saturday detention was just the first part of an insane revenge plan against us, thought up by the creepy school caretakers, the Latchitts. Who also happen to be Colette's grandparents. We'd all made some scrutty choices and hurt Colette at the start of Year 7, and they weren't happy about it. She's forgiven us now and is one of us but the Latchitts haven't. It's hella complicated.

'Well, I'd pick all of you to represent Dread Wood High,' Mr C says loyally. 'And though you may suspect Mr Hume's motives in giving you this responsibility, I'm confident that he selected you because he sees you as assets to the school.'

He does his best to look convincing but I don't think even Mr C believes it.

'Now let's save our best choccie chat for the main event and focus on getting everything prepared for the visitors. I'm heading to the dining-hall kitchens to fill the urns for the hot beverages and load the refreshment trolley . . .'

'Ooh, there's a refreshment trolley?' Gus's eyes light up.

'Could you lot set out the chairs around the tables and have a general tidy?' Mr C says. 'Then come across to the kitchens in fifteen minutes to help carry everything back here? And yes, there will be biscuits for everyone who manages to get through the evening without mentioning helter-skelters being set on fire or stealth attacks in the girls' toilets.'

'Yessssss!' Gus does a little dance.

'Poggers,' Mr C says, and claps his hands while we all groan. 'I'm off before you can throw cushions at me.' He starts jogging towards the door. 'And remember: fifteen minutes, in the kitchens.'

'Biscuits for everyone and an after-hours peek in the secret domain of the dinner ladies.' Gus rubs his hands together. 'And there was us thinking that being at school on a Thursday night would be all boredom and misery.'

We finish our drinks and then laugh at Gus's attempts at rapping while we drag chairs across the room and arrange them around tables. It's full dark outside which makes it feel much later than it is, and I'm suddenly aware of the strangeness of being in school at night. There's none of the usual noise and movement. No slamming doors, ringing bell, students chatting, teachers shouting.

'What time is it?' I say, because I have no idea.

Naira looks at her watch. 'Six forty-five.'

'What time were we supposed to meet Mr C in the kitchen?'

'Fifteen minutes,' Gus says, looking proud that he remembered.

'Yeah but from when?' I say. 'Anyone know?'

'Oops,' Colette says. 'I didn't check.'

'Neither did I.' Hallie sits on the arm of one of the sofas. 'What time did we get here? Wasn't it five thirty?'

'Yeah.' I nod. 'And that feels like ages ago.'

'Can't have been that long or Mr C would have come and got us, surely?' Gus says, but in a way that makes me think he's doubting himself.

'Yeah, why wouldn't he have come back?' Hallie stands up slowly, and I wonder if the others are feeling the creeping claws of dread prickling through their stomachs like I am. We've been through enough at this school to suspect the worst whenever anyone goes missing for more than a minute.

'We should go.' Colette's already heading for the door.

'Right behind you,' Naira says.

And the rest of us follow. Out of student services and into the biting cold of the October night, our breath hanging in the air like it's waiting for something.

CHAPTER TWO

JURASSIC KITCHEN

We follow the path around the modern building that houses student services and the humanities classrooms, and head towards the older part of the school. The mansion. The mansion is like something out of a haunted house movie – all creaky wooden staircases, dark nooks and the heads of long-dead stags hanging on the walls. There are tons of stories about weird stuff happening there – strange screams in the night and footsteps along empty corridors. But we've met way worse things than ghosts there.

It's that part of the year between autumn and winter when I'm still resisting wearing my big coat and pretending not to shiver when my mum insists that I must be cold. It's a battle we have every year, and I will stretch it out for as long as I can. The sharp air stings my nose, overpowering the mulchy smell that always drifts over from the Dread Wood. As we reach the corner of the classroom block, the front of the school stretches ahead of us — most of it huddled in darkness but with a hub of light and activity from the car park to the main foyer where the visitors are entering in small groups. They move fast to get out of the cold, and the entrance sucks them into its pool of light like a hungry mouth slurping crouton-spotted soup. The foyer leads to the assembly hall where Mr Hume will soon be giving a speech about the wonders of Dread Wood High.

'Front way or back way?' Naira says through clenched teeth. I guess she's feeling the chill too.

'Don't want to run into sussy Hume,' Gus says. 'So back way.'

'Yeah.' Colette holds back the curls of her hair that are blowing into her face. 'Definitely.'

When we got back from the trip to France, we promised Mr C that we'd keep out of Hume's way. The guy is one hundred per cent up to some seriously bad stuff, and we're desperate to find out if he's been working with the Latchitts. But we also know we have to be careful, because if he is on Team Latchitt then he probably wants us out of the way for good. And now is not the time for a showdown. So we turn away from the reassuring glow of the foyer and take the path that passes the arts and science blocks and will lead us to the smaller entrance of the dining hall.

'Mr C probably got called away to deal with something and is running behind.' Hallie breaks the silence suddenly, confirming that she's worrying about the same thing that I am. I think all of us are stressing about our favourite teacher.

'Oh god, Hallie's trying to look on the positive side,' Gus says. 'That's got to be an end-of-the-world omen.'

'We do all tend to jump straight to the worst-case scenario,' Naira says. 'But there must be hundreds of reasonable explanations for Mr Canton not coming back, and most of them won't involve anything awful.'

'You sure about that, Nai-Nai?' Gus says. "Cos your mouth is saying the words, but I can see your ponytail twitching like it's about to go full Fright Hair on Elm Street again.'

'Why does it always come back to my hair?' Naira says. 'Either that or cannibalism.'

'Because we live in uncertain times, Naira.' Gus pats her on the shoulder. 'And your hair and cannibalism are our only constants.'

As we get further behind the school buildings, the darkness around us grows. Across the field I can see the shadowy trees in the Dread Wood looming, skeletal branches reaching into the navy sky. The wind gusts through the spaces between the school buildings, whistling in a way that, for a second or two, reminds me of Mr Latchitt whistling nursery rhymes. The way the Latchitts use nursery rhymes as part of their experiments is creepy – controlling their creations with old-fashioned tunes in unexpected ways. I can't hear any kind of childhood song now without shuddering. But that's what the Latchitts do – they take wholesome things and twist them into nightmares.

Then the dining-hall door is in front of us and as Hallie pulls it open, light floods out and I figure that Naira is right – we do always fear the worst. The Latchitts are locked up. There's no need to think something bad has happened.

'Mr C!' Hallie yells out, making the rest of us jump. Her shout bounces off the walls and echoes around the hall.

'Jeez, Hal, a little warning next time, maybe?' Colette says. 'Not loving the jump scares right now.'

'We're not going to find him by whispering, are we?' Hallie walks into the centre of the room and looks around. The lunch tables and benches are stacked in one corner. The floor squeaks from its after-lunch mopping. It's weird being there without the usual smell of pizza slices and apple crumble.

'Looks like we'll have to go into the kitchen then,' Gus says, as if he's been waiting for this moment all his life, and he runs like an excited puppy to the door that leads to the serving area. He pushes it too hard and it swings open, smashing into the wall on the other side with a crash that sounds harshly loud in the quiet of the hall. Then it slams back into place, shutting Gus away from the rest of us.

We hear a shrill scream from behind the door – the kind of scream that only Gus can make – and we run towards it, barrelling into the door so that it smashes into the wall again. We skid across the tiled floor and crash into Gus, who is staring at one of the walls.

'What the hell?' Hallie says, grabbing his arm.

I spin around to look where he's looking, expecting to see a ransom message for Mr C smeared over the pale blue wall in blood. Or something like that at least.

'What is it, Gus?' Colette says. 'What happened?'

'Oh god,' Naira sighs. 'It's the dinner lady uniforms, isn't it?'

'Look at them,' Gus whispers. 'They're just hanging there.'

'And you're going to try on one of the hats.' Naira walks over to a row of long pink and white button-up coats hanging from pegs, with matching caps perched neatly on top. She takes one of the hats and passes it to Gus.

'You shouldn't encourage him, Naira.' Hallie rolls her eyes.

Gus loves many things – artisan snacks, pointy sticks, laughing at dumb stuff on the internet, and also, randomly, putting on costumes. I've never met anyone so comfortable with standing out, and I love that about him.

Colette giggles as Gus takes the hat and looks at it adoringly.

'It would be rude not to,' he says, placing it carefully on his head and then giving a weird wink and putting on an accent of some kind. 'Morning, duckie, what'll it be for you today?'

'I thought we talked about the winking thing always being a bad idea,' I say, but I'm biting back a grin.

Gus gazes at the kitchens stretched out in front of us, the rows of shiny metal counters glinting under the white strip lights. The layout's like a mirror maze – you can only see the area immediately around you and anything beyond that is hidden. 'So this is where the magic happens.'

'Or where we get pack-hunted by velociraptors.' Colette peers down one of the rows like there might be something lurking in the space between. And it does feel like that. Like we're not alone here. Like there's someone, or something, watching us.

'Let's go.' Hallie starts moving towards the back of the room. ''Cos it's weird that Mr C hasn't popped up to tell us off already.'

'Fine, but I'm wearing the hat.' Gus follows her and then the rest of us – Naira, Colette and me. Single file because the aisle space is narrow, checking down each row for any signs of life.

'Actually, being chased through a professional kitchen is such a cliché,' Naira says. 'I wish they'd stop putting those scenes in movies and TV. It's just lazy writing.'

'Na-ah,' Gus says, running his fingers along a polished countertop. 'Some things become cliché because they're so awesome that people are always happy to see them. They're like a joyful version of a cliché. A gleeché.'

'There's always giant pots of soup, and chefs doing that frying flipping thing where actual flames rise up out of the pan,' Colette says from in front of me.

'And, like, a stupid amount of chopping with the most bad-ass-looking knives,' I say, picturing the kitchen as it would look in an action scene.

'Don't forget the waiting staff carrying impossibly balanced plates of food,' Naira says. 'Piled high and just waiting to be sent crashing down.'

'All adds to the gleeché drama,' Gus says, and I wonder how the scene is playing out in his head. Similar to mine, probably, but about a hundred times more over the top. Wouldn't be surprised if he added a couple of ninjas and a Tyrannosaurus rex.

'Guys,' Hallie says, breaking into a jog. 'Look. The trolley.' She darts forward and turns a corner to a part of the kitchens that's tucked away in a separate section. On the counter there are three metal canisters the size of fire extinguishers, lids flipped open.

Gus puts his hand over the top of one. 'Still warm,' he says. 'Meaning Mr C hasn't been gone for long.'

'Of course they're still warm.' Naira rolls her eyes. 'They're like giant thermos flasks. It's their literal job to keep things warm. Even with the lids open it would take ages for whatever's inside to go cold.'

'What *is* inside?' Gus says, peering into the urn. 'I hope it's not . . .'

Naira nudges him aside and sniffs. 'It's coffee.'

'That's what they want you to think,' Gus mutters quietly and adjusts his dinner lady hat.

'The others are empty,' Colette says. 'And the biscuits are still in packets. So Mr C didn't get a chance to start doing what he was planning to do before leaving.'

'Which is weird,' I say. ''Cos we all know he –'

'Never leaves a job unfinished.' Hallie is looking past the trolley into the corner of the room where a half-open door creaks slightly like it's being moved by a breeze that shouldn't exist, because we're inside and there are no windows in the kitchen.

'Mr C?' I say, hoping hard that he'll poke his head out of the doorway and say something embarrassing. But he doesn't. The door creaks again. I edge past the trolley and walk to the door, because if there is something nasty behind it then we might as well get it over with. I grab the handle and pull it open. It's a walk-in cupboard full of cooking ingredients arranged neatly on shelves. But on the floor . . .

'Come look,' I say to the others, and they step up behind me and peer over my shoulders. At the back of the room there's a slatted grate that's been fitted in among the floor tiles. It's the size of a manhole cover and made of dull, slightly rusted metal which seems out of place against the shininess of the kitchen. And though it's clearly been in place for a very long time, someone has recently moved it – scraping it across the tiles to reveal an opening underneath.

'Is that a freaking trapdoor?' Hallie says.

'It might be if we were at a kids' magic show,' Naira says. 'In big school we call them concealed access points to underground areas.'

'It's a freaking trapdoor,' Colette gasps.

'And someone's opened it in the last hour or so,' I say.

'Angelo is the magician!' Gus says. 'He's using his all-seeing eye to look into the past.'

'No,' I say. 'I'm using my actual eyes to see the ink on the ground that's been smeared into tracks where the grate's been dragged through it. It's still wet.'

They all fall silent, and I reckon their brains are racing through the same thoughts that mine is.

'Mr C's clipboard!' Colette grabs my arm with one hand and point with the other at the clipboard, poking out from underneath one of the shelves like it skidded across the floor.

I pull my phone out of my pocket and turn on the torch, shining it down into the rectangle of dark that used to be hidden beneath the grate. There's a big drop – maybe ten metres, and then a rough stone floor below. And way too conveniently . . .

'There's a ladder.'

'Right.' Naira looks down into the passage. 'So obviously a trap, then.'

'Yeah, obviously,' I say.

But Mr C is clearly down there, and he's one of us. So we all know what we're going to do.

'I'll go first,' I say, lowering myself into the opening, torch gripped tightly in my right hand, the cold smoothness of the ladder biting into the skin of my left one. I test the rungs of the ladder as I go. They're solid, as I knew they would be. And then my feet hit the ground, kicking up a layer of grit and dust, and I shine my torch into the darkness ahead.

CHAPTER THREE

INTO THE DARKNESS

There's a tunnel,' I say. 'Looks like it leads back towards the old part of the school.'

'You mean where the Latchitts' lab was before we blew it up?' Hallie jumps off the ladder and stands next to me.

I think for a moment back to that Saturday detention. And the first time the Latchitts tried to finish us off by unleashing genetically mutated spiders on us. 'Yeah. We never saw beyond the giant spider nest – there must have been more passages. Maybe more labs.'

Gus joins us. 'Blowing up that lab was one of the greatest moments of my life.' He mimes aiming the nail gun he was holding at an invisible oxygen canister. 'Say what you like about the Latchitts – at least they've given us some opportunities that your typical teenager won't ever get to experience.'

'I guess you didn't blow up the lab enough, though.' Colette stands behind us as Naira drops down the last rungs of the ladder.

'I guess we didn't,' I say.

'Not gonna make that mistake again.' Hallie turns on her phone torch and points it down the tunnel, swinging the beam from side to side so that we can see the walls, the ground and the ceiling. If you can call it a ceiling when it's made of roughly hewn rock. The tunnel has clearly been dug out, rather than being a natural passage, but it's nothing fancy like the tunnel we found leading from the school basement. No lights. Definitely a back-up entrance.

Hallie rolls back her shoulders like she's warming up for a fight. 'As soon as we've found Mr C, I'm getting some weapons and I'm gonna do some serious destruction down here.'

'Do you think there are more spiders?' Colette takes her glasses off and wipes them on her sleeve.

'Maybe,' I say.

'Fantastic.' Naira sighs. 'I really hated those spiders.'

'At least I won't feel left out when you talk about them any more,' Colette says. 'I always get a bit of FOMO about it.'

'You might not have been here, but your grandparents' creepy shrine to you was,' Gus says. 'Covered a whole wall in the lab. I've never seen so many spy photos of someone in my life. And that includes my

23

cousin Julia's bedroom and her Gustav collection.'

We all snigger and start making our way down the passage, which is just about high enough to stand up in and wide enough for two people at a time. It smells of dust and wet PE kit that's been left in your bag for a week.

'Pa Latchitt would struggle to fit down here,' Gus says, as we walk – quickly but carefully – into the chilling black ahead of us. I shiver thinking of Mr Latchitt, a giant of a man. He never says much, but the size of him alone is totally terrifying. Our torches help, but the walls aren't smooth – there are cracks, and craters, and overhangs. Plenty of places for something to hide.

'Remember Mrs Latchitt used to help out in the kitchens a lot when they were the caretakers?' Naira says. 'She probably used this tunnel more than he did.'

'Creepy to think of them scurrying around under here while we were all in lessons, or eating lunch, or sitting in assembly.' Colette sounds freaked out, and she has more reason to be than the rest of us, seeing as the Latchitts turned out to be her long lost grandparents.

'Like nasty, sneaky rats,' Hallie says, and she kicks a loose stone which pings off one of the walls and rolls somewhere the light from our torches doesn't reach.

'Hold up.' Naira puts her hand on my shoulder. 'Do you hear that?'

We stop walking.

'Hear what?' Gus says. 'The fiery fury of Halkster's burning rage?'

'Shush a minute,' Naira says.

Gus shuts up.

We stand still and quiet for twenty seconds but don't hear anything except the sound of our own breathing.

'What did it sound like, Nai?' Colette asks. Because if Naira says she heard something then she almost definitely did. She's not the kind of person who lets her imagination run away from her.

Naira frowns. 'I know this will sound stupid, but honestly it was like a baby crying.'

'A human baby, or a spider baby?' Gus asks.

'None of us even know what a spider baby cries like, so how could it be that?' Hallie says. 'She obviously meant a human baby.'

'Let's keep moving,' I say, because I can see this turning into an argument, and we really don't have time. I set off again, straining my ears to hear whatever it was that Naira heard.

'But it's way more likely that there's a spider baby than a human baby down here,' Gus says. 'If we're thinking logically.'

'Maybe genetically mutated giant spider babies

sound the same as human babies,' Colette says with a shrug.

'I can see the end of the tunnel,' Hallie says, jogging off ahead as always. 'It opens out into a cave-type thing.'

'Wait up,' Naira calls after her. 'We should stick together.'

But Hallie disappears around a corner, and while the rest of us run to catch up we hear a scream, and a thud, and what sounds horribly like a phone smashing to the ground.

'Hal?' I rush around the corner and stumble over Hallie, who's scuffling around in the dust in the dark, I assume looking for her phone which is her favourite thing in the world.

'What the hell happened?' Gus asks, offering her a hand. 'Did you trip over your own reckless impulsiveness?'

'Shut up, Gustav,' Hallie says. 'And help me find my phone.'

A horrible cracking sound is followed by a moment of horrified silence.

'Found it,' Gus says. 'It was under my shoe.'

'Give it here.' Hallie sounds like she's going to explode with anger. 'I need the torch.'

'Use mine,' Colette says, passing her phone over.

Hallie grabs it and swings it frantically around the cave, her eyes wide and her hand shaking.

'What is it, Hal?' Naira crouches next to her. Puts her hand on her shoulder.

'I didn't trip,' Hallie whispers, still looking around the room in panic. 'Something crashed into me like a freaking bowling ball.'

'Something like a falling rock?' Naira says.

'It came from the side. And low down,' Hallie growls. 'I don't know what it was but it was a living thing.'

'A spider?' Colette says and I swear she sounds almost hopeful. I guess spider FOMO is a real thing.

'Nah,' Hallie says. 'Not this time. But there's some kind of creature in here with us. It's fast, it's strong and it's salty as hell.'

CHAPTER FOUR

CANNONBALL

We form a huddle, back to back. The four of us with still-working phones holding up our torches like a modern-day version of flaming beacons, and Hallie cracking her knuckles, probably hoping to take out her broken-phone rage on the mystery creature.

I can see now that the cave we're standing in is like the tunnel – it hasn't formed naturally, it's been created by humans. Whether it was made by the Latchitts or someone else, I don't know for sure. But it feels old and makes me wonder what's been going on under our school for the past two hundred years. Don't have to wonder too hard about what the Latchitts were using it for, though.

'Look at those cages,' I say, gazing at the piles of empty, half-mangled crates and cages heaped in piles around the edges of the cave. There are at least forty – different shapes and sizes, some of them with bent bars where whatever was inside has tried to get out. I shine my torch on the stack closest to me and see tooth marks and deep scratches and it makes me shudder. 'We're not the only victims of the Latchitts' cruelty.'

'Poor animals.' Hallie stops cracking her knuckles for a moment and runs her hand over a deep gouge in the side of one of the cages. 'We've been so busy fighting what the Latchitts have turned their experiments into that sometimes I forget that they started out as beautiful creatures.'

'But at least we stopped the Latchitts,' Naira says. 'They can't torture anything or anyone else now.'

'So whatever's down here is from before,' Colette says. 'Something they left behind.'

A noise behind a heap of crates makes us turn to face it.

'If they left it behind,' Gus says, aiming the beam of light from his phone at the wall behind the crates. 'It might be because it's so cute and friendly that they disowned it, right?'

'Gus, it already flattened me,' Hallie says.

'But that's understandable,' Gus says. 'We've all wanted to do that from time to time.'

Hallie spins around to either yell at him or punch him, and something shoots out of the darkness to the left of us – so sudden and so fast that all I see is the blur of a shadow – then it missiles into us, knocking us like skittles and breaking up our huddle.

'What was that?' I say, trying to regain my balance and get a look at our attacker. But it's gone as quickly as it appeared. Then something hits me from behind, sending me crashing on to my knees. I put my hands out to stop my face from smashing into the floor and feel sharp pieces of stone slicing into my palms.

I hear a swear from Colette and she slams to the ground next to me, her elbows taking most of the impact. I hear her suck in a breath, and she stays where she is for a few seconds like she's focusing on dealing with that immediate rush of pain. Then she lets out the breath and sits up. 'Ow.'

I pass her back her dropped phone and we help each other to our feet in time to see Gus, then Naira, then Hallie fall to the ground with bone-crashing thuds. Only one of the torchlights is still shining, and that's currently pointing up Gus's nose.

'We need to get out of here,' I say. 'We can't fight when we don't know what we're fighting and we can't see where it's coming from.'

'I saw an exit,' Naira says. 'Far right wall, behind the alarmingly large and mashed-up cage.'

'Right. Grab your phones if you can find them and re-huddle. We move together.' I help Gus up and spot my cracked phone a metre or so to my left. I'm gutted it's smashed because there's no way my parents can afford to get me a new one, but I guess we have bigger worries right now. Luckily the torch switches on when I press the button, and as I turn to face the exit, I catch a glimpse of something darting into the corner.

'I saw it,' I yell, focusing the glow from my phone into the darkness where it disappeared. But even while I'm looking, I hear a yell from behind me, a swear from Hallie, a scream from Gus, and I know it's struck again. I stop searching for it – reluctantly because I'm desperate to see what it is – and concentrate on looking for the exit.

'Everyone up?' I ask, trying to keep watch on every potential ambushing spot as I plan our route out of the cave.

'For now,' Naira says. 'Let's move.'

And we stumble through the dark, around the obstacles in our path, and towards the only way out of this room that isn't the way we came in. None of us even suggests going back to the kitchens. We're not leaving without Mr C.

'Let's hope there's a freaking light switch through that doorway,' Hallie says. 'And some weapons.'

'Gonna find me a good ol'-fashioned pointy stick.' Gus is breathing heavily, and I realise that I am too – I'm sweating and out of breath and we can only have been down here for about fifteen minutes.

'And we're back to fantasising about weapons again.' Naira sighs. 'We end up in these situations way too often. Any movement your side, Angelo?'

'Yeah, I got it,' I say, catching the tip of a shadow darting away from my torchlight and back towards the far side of the room. This is our chance. 'Go now!'

And we huddle-run to the arch-shaped alcove that Naira found, and I'm hoping that there really is a doorway there, and that it leads somewhere useful, or we're all going to end up badly hurt.

'I see a door,' Colette says and I hear the screech of old metal as she pushes it open. We spill through into the space behind it, tripping over each other and ending up in a heap.

'Someone shut it so the cannonball can't chase us,' Gus gasps, and I realise he can't shut it because I'm lying on one of his legs. I scramble to get myself up, but then there's a crackle, and a flicker, and a light pings on – too bright after the darkness of the cave. I instantly screw my eyes closed, then try to force them open so I haven't just replaced dark blindness with light blindness. We need to know if we're still in danger. I manage to squeeze them open enough to give me a tiny, slit-sized view of the area around me, and I catch a glimpse of a grey feathered creature speeding past us and disappearing into a white glare so bright that I can't focus on it.

'Damn it,' Hallie says. 'Can anyone see enough to shut the door?'

'I'm not sure it matters,' I say. 'Whatever was in there with us has come out with us and run off somewhere.'

But then I hear the squeak of hinges and a slam loud enough to make the air vibrate.

'It auto-closed,' Gus says. 'Which ranks high on the horror movie vibe scale.'

He's right. And it probably means that the feathery creature was trapped in there until we let it out. I'm relieved to be away from the dark cages – they made me feel all kinds of uncomfortable – but now I'm worried that our route back to the kitchens has been blocked off and that there's an unidentified something running around down here with us.

'Are you sure it's gone?' Colette says, and I can just about make out the shape of her in front of me, sitting up and rubbing her eyes behind her glasses. 'Cos we're kind of vulnerable right now.'

'Yeah, we're like sleeping ducks,' Gus says.

'It's sitting ducks, Gustav,' Naira sighs.

'I know we're in a bad sitch, but there's no need to swear, Nai-Nai,' Gus says.

'You know I said "sitting", so I'm not going to even bother rolling my eyes,' Naira says.

'But what's with the duck stuff anyway?' Hallie asks. And as whatever the cannonball creature was seems to have left the immediate area, it's nice to have some chat while we try to get our breath back and our sight back, and rub our bruised knees. 'There are loads of things that are more vulnerable than ducks. Like supply teachers at the end of term, or the kids that come in on mufti days wearing school uniform.'

I squeeze my eyes tight shut and then try to open them properly again. After a few blinks I finally manage to get a proper look around us. We're in a corridor – not a tunnel or a passage, but a smooth, painted corridor. There are electric lights evenly spaced along the ceiling, and from where I'm sitting, at least four different doors leading off to who knows what.

'It's definitely gone,' I say. 'Maybe it has a pack somewhere down here.'

'Excellent news,' Naira says. She's looking around at the spookily clinical corridor with its anonymous doors. 'Definitely Latchitt territory.'

'Did the other lab smell like this?' Colette stands up and she's holding one of her arms in a sling-like position, tucked inside her blazer.

'Your elbow?' I say, and she nods.

'The labs smell like your elbow?' Gus says, wiping grit off his hands on to the legs of his trousers. 'Actually, backtrack that: you have an elbow smell? I thought I was supposed to be the weird one of the group.' He lifts his right arm and twists his elbow towards his nose, sniffing deeply.

'I was checking to see if Col's hurt her elbow,' I say. 'Which she has. The smell is a separate issue.'

Naira goes to Colette. 'Can I see? If it hurts that much we should probably take a look at it.'

Colette goes to shrug and then squeaks with pain as her arm moves with her shoulders. By the time we've helped her get her blazer off, her eyes are filled with tears that she's fiercely trying to hold back. I can see the scar on her brow where the vampire birds attacked us in the summer.

'It's not bleeding,' Naira says eventually. 'But it's already swelling. We need to get it in a proper sling. Does anyone have anything we can use?'

We look around. Rummage in our pockets. But of course none of us has anything because we were supposed to be looking our smartest in pristine school uniforms.

'Sorry, Col,' Gus says. 'Next time we come into an

underground lair we need to make sure we're more prepared. I tell you what – I'll let you have the squashed Mars bar I've been saving in my pocket.'

Colette snorts out a laugh. 'I'll be fine, don't worry.'

'There's got to be something in one of these rooms that we can use,' Hallie says, looking up and down the corridor. 'I mean, I don't know if evil villains are first-aid kit kind of people, but they must have some rope, or gags . . .'

'Or one of Ma Latchitt's headscarfs,' Gus says. 'She was a big headscarf fan, remember? Always giving off the witchy peasant vibes.'

'I don't care how much my arm hurts.' Colette is struggling back into her blazer. 'I am not using something that's been on Mrs Latchitt's head to bandage it up.'

'I wonder what it would smell of?' Gus says and I think all of us do a little sick in our mouths.

'Speaking of smells,' Naira says. 'There really is a stench down here. The last Latchitt lab was clean and tidy, but if stuff down here has been left for months without anyone checking on it . . .'

'And especially if the stuff is living animals with no one to clean up after them . . .' I nod.

'It's going to be turd central down here,' Gus says.

I look up and down the corridor. 'So do we want to

take the turds to the right, or the left first?'

'Which way did the vicious creature run?' Colette asks.

'Left,' I say. 'So it would be great if right feels like the correct way to go.'

'Mr Canton?' Colette calls. 'If you're down here and conscious, please give us a sign so we don't have to open every one of these doors and deal with the potential turds behind them.'

We listen for a moment but all I can hear is the faint hum of electricity running through the strip lights.

'Mr C?' Hallie yells.

Again there's no response.

'Are we sure he's down here?' Naira asks. 'What if someone set up the kitchen to make us think he climbed or fell down the ladder, knowing we'd follow?'

'You mean sussy Hume,' Gus says. 'Wouldn't be a shock.'

'But if Hume really does want to get rid of us, then surely he wants to eliminate Mr C too.' Hallie's rolling up the sleeves of her blazer and shirt. 'Hume knows that Mr C knows what's been going on. He's as much of a threat to the whole Latchitt domination plan as we are.'

'But the Latchitts are out of action,' Colette says. 'They're locked up and going to trial soon. Why even bother continuing with whatever they were planning?'

'Makes me worry that he knows something we don't.' I've been thinking it for a while but haven't wanted to freak anyone out. 'It doesn't feel like the danger is over. And maybe that's just me being paranoid 'cos of everything that's happened, but . . .' I shrug.

'I know what you mean,' Hallie says. 'The Latchitts were working with other people. Some of them we know about . . .' She glances at Colette because she's obviously meaning Col's dad. Dad by blood but not any other way. 'But there could be loads that we don't. The Latchitts started this, but maybe someone else wants to finish it.'

'Hold up.' Naira takes a few steps along the corridor to our right and stops. 'I can hear that weird sound again. Listen.'

We stand next to Naira, ears straining to hear what she's hearing. And after a couple of seconds I catch it – a shrill wail, like –

'It *is* a baby crying,' Gus says, and him and Hal run further down the corridor then stop for another listen.

'This way.' Hallie speeds off. 'Come on.'

And that's it. Decision made. We're exploring the labs no matter what, because even if Mr C isn't down here, something else is. And we need to find out what.

CHAPTER FIVE

SCOOBY POO

We jog past four closed doors – two on each side of the corridor. Maybe we'll have to check out what's behind them later, but for now we focus on following the sound.

'How could there be a baby down here?' Colette says. 'What if it's a recording that someone's playing to lure us deeper into this hellhole?'

'Maybe,' Gus says. 'But we have to check, don't we? We can't walk away without knowing. And besides, it sounds real to me.'

'Baby expert, are you?' Hallie says.

'Big family, remember,' Gus says. I notice he's limping – another injury from the cannonballing in the cave by the mystery creature. 'And when we have family parties, the babies get handed around like Halloween candy. Except less tasty and more waah-y. This will probably come as a surprise because of my extreme alpha appearance . . .' We all try not to snigger. 'But I'm skilled in soothing babies. One look at my face and they stop crying. When we find this one, I'll show you.'

'Left,' Naira says, leading the way. She's always the fastest. And we follow her around a corner into a shorter, wider hallway. There's an opening about halfway down that we run towards, slowing down as we reach it in case anything nasty jumps out. There's no door on this one, just an archway that leads to what looks like an enormous cave that's flooded with water.

The crying sounds again – much closer now. And it isn't coming from the lake cave. I turn away and look back down the hallway. There's just one more opening off this corridor, and it's at the very end. No door that I can see again – just a misshapen opening and inky blackness beyond. We walk over to it, and I'm hoping that when we enter we'll find it's been fitted with lights. But there's no flicker. No sound. No movement. When we step beyond the glow leaking in from the lights in the corridor, I'm pretty sure we're going to be completely in the dark again.

'Why have they put lights in some rooms and not others?' I say, my brain scanning through the possibilities. The cunning Latchitts always have a reason for everything. And I wonder if the reason has anything to do with whatever creature has been, and maybe still is, living in here.

'I guess we'll be needing these again.' Colette pulls her phone out of her pocket with her less injured arm and turns on the light.

'Let's just use two phones at a time,' Naira says. 'Save the batteries in case we're down here for a while.'

'Good thinking, Nai.' Gus switches his on too. 'I'll go up front. Colette, you keep watch at our rears. We don't want anything creeping up on us Scooby Doo style. Although actually, we should assign Scooby parts because I'm pretty sure I'm the buff one.'

'You're Scooby,' we all say at the same time.

'Na-ah,' he says. 'On what grounds?'

'Scooby snacks,' we all say at the same time again.

'I'm outraged,' Gus says. 'I am not a Scooby. Would Scooby do this?' And he dance-walks into the pitch-black cave like Peter Parker in *Spider-Man 3*.

'So who would I b–?' Hallie says, following Gus into the cave.

'Scrappy,' the rest of us interrupt, like it's the most obvious thing in the world, because it is.

'Go ahead, Velma.' I nod to Naira to go next while I stay back with Colette and we grin at each other.

'Well, someone has to be the smart one.' Naira raises an eyebrow and walks into the darkness.

'Guess that makes us Daphne and Fred,' Colette says.

41

"Cos Shaggy and Scooby are basically the same person so Gus gets both of those.'

'So are Daphne and Fred,' I say. 'They suck.'

'They do.' Colette nods. 'Whose idea was this anyway?' She shines her torch into the cave.

'Gus's obviously,' I say. 'Let's be the super-evolutions of Fredne.'

'Fredne: Gear Five,' Colette says, and we move forward together, using Gus's torchlight to guide us, and using Col's to illuminate other parts of the space around us. It's another natural cave, but this one is more than just an open room. It has piles of rocks rising from the ground so it's impossible to follow a straight path across. There are bottomless black crevices and shadowy recesses that could be concealing anything. Above us there's a web of branches and what looks like sackcloth fabric strung from edge to edge, forming a kind of canopy over our heads. Like a habitat the keepers would create for an animal in a zoo. And it's this that's making me worry more than anything else. I can't help thinking that there's something up there, watching us.

'That is a smell and then some,' Gus says. 'Like there are layers to it and none of them are minty fresh. Also, the ground is really slippery here, so be careful once you get past the lump of rock that looks like an ice-skating badger.'

'How can a rock look like an ice-skating badger?' Hallie says, and then she swears a bunch of times.

'Told you it was slippy,' Gus says, and I can hear the grin in his voice.

'You know what?' Naira says suddenly, and me and Col freeze, thinking she's heard a sound we haven't, or figured something out about the cave. 'It actually *does* look like an ice-skating badger.'

'Like I said.' Gus is out of sight now, but the cave is so quiet that his words bounce off the walls and echo around us like he's standing at our side.

'For freak's sake, what even is this squelchy stuff?' Hallie says. 'I've slipped in it about a hundred times already and it's all over my trousers.'

Naira makes a noise that sounds a lot like a snigger. 'Remember when we talked about what could be producing the stench, Hal?'

'Yeah . . . oh wait. Oh no.'

'You're walking on a blanket of animal poo.'

'It's a turd carpet, a carpet made from turds,' Gus starts singing.

'But I put my hand in it!' Hallie wails.

And we're laughing hard, even though we should be

43

focusing on the potential dangers around us. Because we can't stop ourselves, and because laughing helps. It always helps.

'Hey, look,' Colette says, once we've calmed down enough to start looking around again. 'There's something hanging off the wall over there.'

I look to the left as she shines the light from her phone on a spot about two metres off the ground, where a rusty cone-shaped object is fixed to the wall, surrounded by a sort of metal cage.

'Hold up, guys,' I call ahead to the others, as we move as fast as we can on the uneven surface over to the wall. 'We've found something.'

As we get close, I can see that it's like an old-fashioned speaker, wired into the rock at the narrow end, the wide end open and facing out into the cave.

'What you got, Scooby gang?' Gus yells. 'Is it old man Marley in a ghost costume?'

'It's a speaker,' I shout to the others, 'with steel mesh around it to protect it.'

'Why would they run electricity cables through the walls but not add lights?' Colette says.

'And why would they put speakers in a cave?' Hallie says from deeper in the cavern.

'I'm more worried about what the steel mesh is

protecting it from,' Naira says. 'Sounds like it's beak and claw proof.'

And that familiar feeling of dread rushes through me because I don't think we're going to like the answers to any of those questions. I squeeze my fingers into the holes in the mesh, and rest my face on it so I can get a better look.

The second I do, it screeches into life, blasting out the sound of static and feedback. I jump backwards and realise that the noise is everywhere, not just around the speaker. And even with the echoes . . .

'There are other speakers,' Colette says. 'All around the cave.'

'This cannot be good,' Hallie yells over the buzzing and squealing. It lasts for a few more seconds then dies down, leaving a moment of painful silence.

And then a horribly familiar voice starts to sing.

'*Rock-a-bye baby on the tree top . . .*'

'Oh god, it's Mrs Latchitt,' Colette gasps. 'Do you think she's here somewhere?'

My heart is pounding so hard that it's making me feel sick and my mouth has gone summer-dirt dry. I can't speak for a second, so I listen to the song to see if I can pick up on anything that might tell us where she is. Because she can't be here. It's not possible.

They're in jail!

'I heard a click at the start of it,' Naira shouts, loud enough that we can hear her over the singing. 'It's a recording.'

And I feel relief, just for a heartbeat or two, before realising that just because she isn't here, it doesn't mean she can't put us through a genetically mutated creature nightmare again. The Latchitts have controlled all of their creations using nursery rhymes, either to draw their creatures in, or prevent them from turning on the Latchitts, or as a signal to attack. If there's a song playing then it's probably going to mean bad things are coming.

'*When the wind blows the cradle will rock . . .*'

And then another sound rings out above us. It's a baby crying. And I can't understand how there could be a baby caught up in the twisted canopy above us, and I'm wondering how we can get up there to save it, but then there's another cry. And another, and another, and another. Until there must be twenty babies wailing.

'*When the bough breaks the cradle will fall . . .*'

And the babies stop crying. There's a pause in the song – it can only be for four or five seconds but it feels a lot longer as dread twists in my gut with the knowledge that something's coming.

'This is bad,' Colette whispers. And I can feel her shaking beside me. I turn to look at her as the last line of the song plays.

'*And down will come baby, cradle and all.*'

Colette's face is pale and scared in the dim light, and I want to tell her that we'll be OK. But then something looms out of the darkness behind her, lunging at her shoulder with its dagger teeth glinting in the torchlight.

CHAPTER SIX

TEETH AND CLAWS

I don't have time to think so I just react, swinging a fist at the gaping mouth before it can sink its teeth into Colette. I feel a crunch as my knuckles connect with its face and then the heat of its teeth gashing the skin on my forearm.

Colette screams and jumps aside, dropping her phone, which smashes on the rocky ground. I don't think any of us are getting out of this with our phones in one piece. She spins around to look at the creature that attacked her, which has fallen back with the impact of my punch. It lands on its feet, just a few metres away, looking ready to pounce again.

It's the size of a large cat. Long-tailed and agile, but it moves more like a primate – a lemur or monkey – using its front paws as hands rather than feet. It has enormous dark eyes. So big that they cover about seventy per cent of its face. And large, pointed ears that twitch, maybe because it's listening, or maybe because it's angry. There's a crackle from however many speakers are hidden around the cave, and then silence, like the recording has glitched. And though the creature keeps swivelling its ears around, it doesn't come any closer.

'It's like a freaky bushbaby,' I say.

'Bushbabies are supposed to be cute, though.' Colette backs up a step, away from the creature and nearer to me. 'That is not cute.'

'It has added mouth,' I say, as it stretches the bottom part of its face into an evil-looking grin, showing those teeth again.

'And claws,' Colette says, and I see that its paws are tipped with curved black claws, at least ten centimetres long.

We stand side by side, eyeballing it while it eyeballs us back. But it's much better at it because it has so much eyeball.

'You guys OK?' I yell over to the others, hoping that they've sat down for a picnic and that's why their torchlight has stopped moving forward.

'Depends on your definition,' Naira calls back. 'You?'

'Same,' Colette shouts.

'Turns out those babies weren't human babies *or* spider babies,' Gus says. 'We should probably re-huddle.'

'Re-huddling sounds like a plan,' I say, as our bushbaby

monster scampers on the spot. Like it's waiting for something. 'How many do you have eyes on?'

'Hold on, let me count,' Hallie yells. There's a few seconds of silence, then, 'We have nine but I think there are more above us. They're blocking us in.'

'We only have one,' Colette says.

'Lucked out there,' Hallie says.

'Are yours smiling at you?' I yell.

'Like the Grinch combo'd with a great white shark,' Gus shouts.

'Any idea why they've crowded around us, Angelo?' Naira shouts. 'They're some kind of mutated bushbaby, right?'

'But bushbabies are supposed to be cute!' Gus says. 'These fellas look like creepy little gremlins. Is nothing sacred to the Latchitts?'

'I think they *are* some kind of bushbaby,' I call back. 'No idea what else has been mixed into their DNA, but there's a good chance that they're nocturnal.'

'So they're staying close to the back of the cave where it's darkest.' Colette bends down slowly, without taking her eyes off the bushbaby, and picks up her phone. And I get it – there's something so reassuring about the weight of a phone in your pocket, even if it's smashed and out of data.

'*Rock-a-bye baby on the tree top . . .*' The damn singing starts playing again, and the bushbaby's ears twitch.

'You guys should run,' Hallie yells. 'You're closer to the exit. Once you get into the light you might be safe.'

'Not without you,' Colette says.

'*When the wind blows the cradle will rock . . .*'

And the bushbaby twists its head to the canopy above and starts howling again. It's so freakishly like a human baby. The others join in too, and the noise is almost overwhelming in the enclosed space.

'You need back-up,' I shout. 'We meet in the middle and we all get out of here together.'

'*When the bough breaks the cradle will fall . . .*'

The bushbabies stop crying, and the one in front of us tenses, ready to attack.

'To the ice-skating badger!' Gus whoops, and Col and I dart towards the rock formation, hoping the others are doing the same from the other side. I scan the area for weapons – anything that will help us fight them off. The only rocks big enough to be of any use are attached to the ground or too heavy to lift. And everything else is just poo. Apparently caves are rubbish if you need something to defend yourself against a pack of genetically modified primates.

Then my foot lands on something hard, which crunches under the sole of my shoe, and I feel a moment of hope that I might have come across something I can use. I shine the torch downwards for a moment and the light falls on a mound of bones. There are piles of them scattered across the ground – picked clean of flesh and sucked empty of juices so all that remains are dry white skeletons.

'They've been eating rats,' I yell. 'They're probably hungry.'

'Perfect,' Hallie says. 'Damn carnivores.'

The bones are too small to fight with, so I look up instead and see a low-hanging branch poking out of the canopy above. I jump for it, aware of the seconds ticking by annoyingly fast, and hang from it with all my weight until part of it snaps off in my hand.

'*And down will come baby, cradle and all.*'

And they attack. Not just our OG critter, but a whole bunch of them, dropping down from the canopy like furry ninjas with built-in shurikens. Some of them land on the ground, some perch on the rock formations, and some go straight for us. I stumble forward as one of them lands on my back, attaching itself to me with its claws like it's a little kid clinging on for a piggyback. Its teeth gnash at my neck as I spin and fling myself backwards into a pile of rock, trying to knock it off. The first hit makes it screech but doesn't detach it, so I try again, flinging myself into the rock so hard that the impact reverberates through my chest and knocks the breath out of me. I feel its claws jerk out of my shoulders, so I take the chance to jump to my feet.

Just ahead of me, Colette is using her good arm like a tennis racket, batting the creatures away. They're strong, and she's injured, so they don't go far before piling on again. I give her my branch and jump up for another one, coming away with what's more like a large stick this time, but it's better than nothing.

Mrs Latchitt's nursery rhyme replays as soon as it ends, and I know that as long as she keeps singing, things aren't going to get any easier. If we could destroy the speakers, we might be able to stop the attack, but I can't locate them in the dark and beyond the tree-branch canopy.

We keep moving forward as fast as we can, Col swinging her branch, and me using my stick like an inadequate spear. The babies go flying but are up and attacking again in seconds. And there are so many of them. I feel the slice of their claws more than once. Finally the ice-skating badger is looming over us and I hear Hallie, Gus and Naira fighting just the other side of it. Hallie is raging and swearing like an angry bull. The others are unusually quiet. They must be struggling.

We rush past the badger to see Hal, Gus and Nai totally surrounded by bushbabies that are flying at them in twos and threes, so fast that they don't have time to take a breath between attacks. They look wrecked.

Colette and I charge forward with our weapons, trying to break through the circle of primates. Hallie goes at them in the same spot while Naira and Gus try to deal with the ones flying in from the side.

'*Rock-a-bye baby on the tree top*,' Mrs Latchitt sings.

'They'll all howl on the next line,' I yell. 'That's our chance to get out.'

'Got it,' Naira shouts, trying to shake off a creature that's latched on to her arm with its teeth. It must sting like a beast.

'I'm so ready to leave this cave,' Gus says. I can see blood seeping through the white of his shirt.

'*When the wind blows the cradle will rock . . .*'

The babies pause. Opening their mouths to wail in that horrific way that will definitely be replayed in my future nightmares if we make it out of this place. And we run. As fast as we can around the rock formations, skidding over the slimy ground, scattering rat skulls. If one of us falls, someone helps them up.

'*When the bough breaks the cradle will fall . . .*'

The crying stops and there's movement behind us. They're chasing us, getting ready for the next round.

'The corridor lights are out,' Hallie shouts. We keep running. 'What if they don't come back on?'

'They'll come back on,' Naira says. 'As soon as we get through the exit.'

I hope she's right.

With no glow from the exit, the bushbabies are bounding and swinging to the front of the cave with us. If at least one of us can get out there and activate the sensors, it will give us a chance.

'*And down will come baby, cradle and all.*'

I fall forward as a bushbaby flies from the canopy and sinks its claws into my scalp. I drop my branch to try to wrench its paws off me. Through blood, sweat and stinking grey fur I see Gus run back to help me.

'Keep moving if you can, Angelo,' he says. 'We're so close.'

'If anyone can get out, get out,' I shout. 'Get the lights on and they should back off.'

'On it,' Naira yells. And I feel less panicked for a second because I know she'll get it done.

But the bushbaby wraps an arm around my neck and I'm finding it hard to breathe. I keep wrestling with it, trying to prise the arm off me, but I can't get a breath in.

'Keep fighting, Angelo,' Gus says. 'Death by bushbaby is an embarrassing way to go.'

And I want to laugh even as my eyes fill with stars and an overpowering rush of heaviness surges through me. But I can't get the laugh out. And then there's just . . . nothing.

CHAPTER SEVEN

STOLEN BISCUIT BREAK

I open my eyes and have to close them again straight away – the white light glaring into them is so bright.

'Don't worry, Angelo, you're in the corridor under school, not Valhalla.' Gus's voice drifts over from somewhere nearby. 'It's fine to go towards the light.'

I smile but keep my eyes closed for a few more seconds, enjoying the feeling of my nose and mouth sucking in oxygen and filling my lungs. My neck and throat hurt like they've been pummelled by a cheese grater, but that's OK. I'm still here. Still breathing.

'Everyone else all right?' I whisper, my voice weak and scratchy.

'All bruised, bleeding, potentially have rabies, but alive and eating biscuits.' Naira's voice sounds reassuringly 'sick of this same old stuff' normal and I allow myself one more second of lying still before I open my eyes and sit up.

'We have biscuits?'

'Nicked them off the trolley before we came down,' Gus says, passing me a party ring, which I shove into my mouth whole before remembering that every part of my body hurts and I probably should have taken a smaller bite.

'I'm starting to worry about your life of petty crime.' Naira is tying what looks like a shirtsleeve around Gus's shoulder as tightly as she can. He's sitting, shirtless, his torso a mess of blood and puncture holes.

'Stupid monkeys missed my bag, so joke's on them.' Gus grins at me and points at the bag connected to his stoma. It's like a pouch of flesh-coloured plastic that sits against his belly and collects the bodily waste that other people would poo out. 'Otherwise the smell out here would be as bad as the smell in there. Club Loser for the win.' I've never seen him without a top on before because he's so self-conscious about his bag, and I'm glad that he seems OK with us seeing it. I don't want to stare though, so I focus on the biscuits.

'And look, he got your favourites,' I say to Naira, passing her a pink one with yellow patterns. She wipes her hands on her trousers and takes it.

'So pretty.' She grins at Gus. 'Thank you.'

'Anything for you, Nai-Nai.' He puts what's left of

his shirt back on – a bloodstained, torn, sleeveless gilet type thing – and fastens his tie around his head like a commando headband, then puts his dinner lady hat on top. 'I don't need a mirror to tell me that I am slaying in this 'fit,' he grins.

'Where are Col and Hallie?' I ask.

'Patched up and scouting the area, but only after I made them promise not to open any doors or go through any dark archways into caves,' Naira says. Her forearms are tied with strips of shirt too, from wrist to elbow. 'I got some bites,' she says. 'We all did.'

'So we reached the ripping-off-pieces-of-our-own-clothes-to-use-for-first-aid-purposes part of the adventure.' Gus crunches on another biscuit. 'I can't believe we've never done it before.'

'Is it as easy as it looks to rip strips of shirt?' I say, feeling bad and also kind of jealous that mine is still in one piece.

'So hard,' Gus says. 'But we have a Hallie and nothing was going to stop her.'

'Angelo!' I look up to see Hallie and Colette jogging up the corridor. Colette's arm is tied up in a neat sling made from the bottom of her shirt from the looks of it, 'cos it's untucked and flapping like a crop top. Her tie has been used to bandage one of her ears. Hallie's arms are wrapped like Naira's. And for some reason she's ripped the bottoms of her trousers off so they're like knee-length shorts.

'Hey!' I smile. 'I pass out for, like, one minute and you all try out a new look without me.'

'Club Loser fashion at its best,' Gus whoops.

'Looks like your right arm needs bandaging.' Naira points at a fresh trail of blood that rolls down my hand and splatters on the ground. 'We're going to need another shirtsleeve.'

I take off my blazer and Hallie uses her teeth and pent-up rage to tear the sleeves off my shirt. I have some deep gouges from the teeth of the first bushbaby that tried to bite Colette, and about a hundred other scratches and bruises. But soon I'm patched up by Naira and feeling like I can get going again.

'Find anything on your mission?' Gus says.

'We found this.' Colette takes something out of her pocket and hands it to him.

'Mr C's pen,' Gus says. 'So he must be down here somewhere – we have to keep searching.'

'We can't go back anyway,' Hallie says. 'The door that automatically shut behind us when we made it out of the cannonball entrance hall will not automatically unshut. We could try levering it open, but it's pretty solid.'

'So we'll find another way out,' Colette says. 'Once we've got Mr C.'

'Ah, we've reached the things-go-from-bad-to-worse part of the adventure,' Gus says. 'At least this one we've been through before.'

'Yeah, we know this one well,' Naira sighs. 'How annoyingly predictable.'

'We've got this.' I stand up, boosted by the sugar rush and knowing that everyone's OK. 'The Latchitts planned for everything – there's got to be other ways in and out.'

'There's the well in the Latchitts' old garden,' Hallie says. 'If we can find it.'

'Good thinking, Halster.' Gus stands up too, and starts doing lunges. 'Angelo will be able to find it – dude has Google Maps for a brain.'

Naira dusts the crumbs off her clothes, which is funny because they're a mess of blood and bushbaby poo anyway. 'We'll have to find a way to climb up, but as long as one of us makes it then we can get everyone out. While we're looking for Mr C, we can also search for rope or anything else we can use.'

'We found Mr C's pen outside a room left of the entrance tunnel,' Colette says. 'So we should start there.'

'A room with a proper door?' I ask. 'So potentially also lights?' Because if I'm going to have to walk blind into another pitch-black cave, I want to make sure I'm mentally prepared.

'Looked like a normal room from the outside.' Hallie shrugs. 'So all signs point to yes. But you never know with the Latchitts, do you?'

'Always keeping a naughty little tricksy up our sleeves, sweetlings,' Gus says in a perfect impersonation of Mrs Latchitt's voice.

'That was amazing,' Colette says. 'Please don't ever do it again.'

We start walking up the corridor, back to where we started about an hour ago, and I am not sad to be saying goodbye to it.

'But I was gonna start my own Latchitt tribute act so I can perform their greatest hits at the next Dread Wood High talent show. "Incy Wincy", "Pop Goes the Weasel". All the bangers.' Gus opens his mouth like he's going to start singing.

'Don't you dare,' Colette squeals. 'I mean it, Gustav.'

'But I've been practising!' Gus says.

'At least don't sing them down here,' Naira says. 'You never know what's listening, and I don't want to get jumped on by any leftover spiders or vamps.'

'She makes a good point,' Hallie says.

'Fine, I'll save them for later,' Gus sighs.

'Or save them for never.' Colette stink-eyes him.

My school uniform is trashed. My hair is crusted with dried blood. I'm painfully thirsty. My whole body hurts, inside and out. And my phone is smashed. But as I follow my friends into who knows what, I break into a massive grin. No matter what happens, my life is so much better now that I'm part of Club Loser.

'You could do a mash-up of the two Karen tunes,' I say. '"Row, row" and "Fish Alive".'

'Ooh, yes.' Gus claps his hands.

'Ooh, no!' Colette turns and glares at me. 'Stop encouraging him, Angelo.' I grin back at her and she can't help breaking into a smile.

Hallie comes to a stop outside an ordinary-looking door. 'This is the place.'

We gather around, inspecting it for anything that might lead us to believe there's a bloodthirsty monster behind it. But it's just a standard wooden door. Painted green. A shiny brass handle to open it, and a few scuffs at the bottom where it's been foot-nudged in day-to-day use.

'Nothing about it screams "ENTER AND DIE",' Colette says.

Naira puts her ear to it and listens.

'Any signs of life?' I ask.

She shakes her head.

We look at each other. Time to get this done.

'Here we go then,' Hallie says. She takes a deep breath and pushes the door open.

CHAPTER EIGHT

THE LAB

The room beyond the green door is dark and still. I take a step inside and nothing changes.

'Why aren't the lights coming on?' Hallie says. 'I don't know if I have the patience to explore another Latchitt party room in the dark. I prefer fights where I can see what's trying to kill me.'

'Even if it's a demonic-looking bushbaby?' Gus says.

'Yes. There's nothing I'd rather not see.'

'Even if it's a giant bird with red eyes and blood dripping from its beak?'

'Yes. Anything.'

'Even if it's –' Gus says.

But then there's a click, and the area floods with bright electric light.

'Light switch.' Colette nods at a panel at the side of the door.

'The Latchitts are so confusing with their use of technology,' Naira says. 'Sometimes they're all deepfakes and state-of-the-art submersible drones. And other times they're old-school speakers and light switches. I wish they'd stick with one way or the other.'

'But it's for the dramz, Nai-Nai,' Gus says. 'You've got to respect their attention to horror movie gleeché detail.'

Hallie rolls her eyes and walks into the room, which is clearly a laboratory like the one we found behind the school basement. But this one is bigger, with multiple doors leading off into cupboards or other rooms. I can't see or hear anything moving around in any of them, but that doesn't mean there's nothing there.

'Stick together this time?' Colette says.

'Yeah.' I nod. 'Splitting up always ends badly.'

The main lab is around the same size as the science labs in school, with rows of counters holding equipment, some that I recognise – like a centrifuge, light boxes and microscopes – and a load of complex-looking stuff that I don't. There are enormous glass containers lined up in rows, each one full of coloured liquid and strangely distorted animal body parts. The fluid is thick and cloudy, so it's hard to make out exactly what's inside, but I peer into one and see what looks like an octopus arm but with spikes instead of suckers. God knows what the Latchitts were busy cooking up in here. There's an empty table in the middle of the room beside a wheeled trolley. In the trays of the trolley are scalpels and swabs and other surgical tools.

'You think they dissect dead animals and stuff on this?' Gus whispers, staring at the array of sharp objects in front of us.

'There are restraining straps,' Naira points out. 'For holding things down. I think they do a lot more than dissecting dead animals on this table.'

'They're freaking monsters,' Hallie says.

Looking at it makes me feel sick, and I can tell the others are feeling the same way, so we move on quickly. I try to put the scalpels out of my mind.

There's a whole wall-length counter of computer equipment and monitors, with printouts and charts that even Naira can't decode.

'The Latchitts are scary smart, aren't they?' I say. 'Like genuine evil genius smart.'

Naira picks up an A4-sized hardback journal and opens it to the first page. 'I know we've destroyed some of their creations, and survived the nightmare situations they've put us in. But it never really feels like we've beaten them.'

'What you're forgetting, Nai-Nai,' Gus says, 'is that I've been working out and am basically Dread Wood High's version of The Rock now. So whatever comes next, we'll win. The Rock never loses. Never.'

Naira looks up and smiles, like she's shaken off her fear – at least for now. 'That's true. Burning skyscrapers, rampaging monsters, earthquakes, ancient curses – he always comes out on top.'

'And in a violent yet wholesome way that makes the world feel like a safer place with him in it.' Colette nods.

'I should change my name to The Gus, shouldn't I?' Gus says.

'Probably not.' I pat him on the shoulder.

'Definitely not.' Hallie snorts. 'There's no way you can pull that off.'

'There's some notes about the bushbabies in here,' Naira says, running her finger over a page of the book. 'It says their vulnerability to bright light and reluctance to venture from their habitat means they're not suitable for field-testing. The Latchitts considered them a failure.'

'A failure that took us down to about half HP,' Gus says, rubbing his chest where the worst of his wounds is.

'What about an angry, rapid, cannonball thing with feathers?' I ask.

'Nothing yet, but I'll keep looking.' Naira closes the drawer but keeps the notebook with her. 'We need to try all the side doors.'

We walk to the first door and brace ourselves for potential disaster when we open it. But when the door swings back we find ourselves looking into a small bathroom.

'Thank god,' Gus says, stepping inside and closing the door on the rest of us. 'I'm dying for a wee. Be out in two mins.'

'You think it's safe to drink water from the tap?' I say, because the thirst I felt outside the bushbaby cave is getting unbearable.

'The bathroom probably uses the same water pipes as the school.' Naira shrugs, still reading the notebook. 'So I'm about ninety per cent certain it'll be fine.'

'Tastes fine to me!' Gus calls from the bathroom where it sounds like he's lapping up water like a dog. 'However, I have bad news about the hand cream . . . It's lavender. Don't touch it unless you want to smell like an old lady.'

We take it in turns to use the toilet and drink from the tap, and honestly the water tastes beautiful.

The next door in the lab leads to a storage cupboard. The third one takes us into a room filled with bits of animals floating in jars like pickled onions. It's disgusting and creepy and we don't stay in there long. Then there's another walk-in cupboard that has floor-to-ceiling fridges full of test tubes containing different-coloured liquids, and labelled phials of chemicals.

The fourth door is right at the back of the main room. And I guess we've been lulled into a false sense of security because when I turn the handle and push it open, I'm expecting another cupboard, or at the very worst some specimens of body parts. I'm not expecting it to be another large room – the light from the lab seeping in far enough to show us that it stretches back for at least ten metres. But what really shocks me is the heat that blasts into my face, like when you come out of an air-conditioned supermarket into forty-degree sunshine. So hot that it's hard to breathe.

'Oh god, another smell.' Gus gags on it as it hits with the heat. It's even worse than the cave – turd-carpety but also rotten and maggoty.

Something rustles beyond where the light reaches. There's something alive in here.

'Hit the lights!' I shout, and then something barrels into my knees, knocking me into Naira who's right behind me. We smash to the ground and I hear a thunk as what I think is Naira's head slams into the door frame.

Hands reach down to help us up, and I grab Hallie's at the same moment that the light clicks on. There's no sterile white glare this time – the room fills with a gentle yellow glow that might feel comforting if I hadn't just had the air knocked out of me by an unknown attacker.

An unknown attacker that's disappeared behind a strange, twisted structure in the middle of the room.

'Was it the cannonball again?' Gus asks.

'Felt like it,' I nod, still trying to get my breath back.

Naira is dazed, her hand on the back of her head while Colette loosens Nai's ponytail and checks her scalp for lumps and cuts. 'No blood,' Colette says. 'But a lump the size of an egg.'

'Perfect,' Naira sighs.

'What is this room?' Hallie says, gazing around. 'And why is it so damn hot?'

I look around, trying to take everything in and add it up in a way that makes sense. The room is square, as wide as it is deep, and has evenly spaced racks wrapped around all of the walls, from the left of the doorway all the way to the right.

The lowest rack is about fifty centimetres from the floor, the next fifty centimetres above that, then another fifty centimetres above that, and carrying on up to the ceiling. The walls aren't painted like the rest of the lab, but kind of padded. So is the ceiling. Aside from the spotlights dotted around above us, there's a huge heat lamp at least a metre in diameter. And the structure in the middle . . . It looks like it's made of shredded trash – cardboard, paper and bits of plastic, even. It's bowl shaped, with staggered sides that rise in steps, high enough that I can't see inside from where I'm standing. It's been built directly under the heat lamp.

A whirr and a click from multiple places hidden in the walls and ceilings tells me that there are speakers here too.

'Oh god,' Hallie says, and we automatically move closer together.

Then the whistling starts. And it's the same whistling that haunts my most terrifying nightmares and wakes me up in sweat-soaked blankets at least once a week.

'Mr Latchitt,' I say. 'But what nursery rhyme is it?'

'Hold on, I think I've got it,' Colette says, as the structure in the middle of the room starts to shake ominously. She hums along for a few seconds, then starts fitting the words into the melody: *'There once was an ugly duckling . . .'*

'This room is an incubator,' I say. 'And that . . .' I point at the structure in the middle of the room, 'is a nest.'

CHAPTER NINE

DINNER TIME

'You think Mr C is in the nest?' Hallie says, looking ready to dive right in.

'They're going to eat him, semi-digest him, then sick him into their babies' mouths!' Gus gasps dramatically. 'I've seen it on TV.'

'I think that's owls,' Colette says. 'But either way, we need to see inside that nest. If Mr C's in there, he must be in bad shape.'

'We run to the nest together, climb up high enough that we can see inside,' I say, and I tense my muscles, ready to move.

But before we make it two steps closer, a stream of the strangest birdlike creatures I've ever seen come swarming over the rim of the nest and form their own huddle in front of us. We skid to a stop and try to take in the sight before our eyes.

'What the actual?' Hallie says.

'Those are some really ugly ducklings.' Colette puts her uninjured hand on my arm. 'What even are they?'

'I have no idea,' I say, my eyes fixed on them. 'But I'm

ninety-nine per cent sure that they're the same as the guy who attacked us in the cage room.' They're about a metre high, with duck-shaped bodies, but bigger and more powerful. Thicker legs built for running fast. And they're mostly bald with scaly grey skin and bristly feathers in patches on their wings and tails, and the tops of their heads.

'Isn't it obvious?' Gus says. 'The Latchitts have gone full *Jurassic Park* and brought back freaking dinosaurs.'

'No way, Gus,' Naira says. 'That's not possible.'

'Listen,' Gus says. 'I've seen ducks and I've seen dinosaurs. And I can say with absolute certainty that those are dinoducks, no duckosaurs. No, Tyrannoducks. No . . . wait! Duckoraptors.'

The duckoraptors watch us with black pool-ball eyes, heads swaying on muscular necks.

'You haven't seen dinosaurs,' Naira sighs. 'Movies don't count.'

'Seen 'em in books too,' Gus says. 'And you love books, Nai-Nai, so I know you're not going to say they don't count.'

'But those pictures are just examples of what scientists think they might have looked like, Gustav. They're not photos.'

'Scientists are smart,' Gus says. 'So it's good enough

for me.'

'I think they're guarding the nest,' I say. 'Just gonna try something a sec.'

I dart forward with no warning, hoping to at least get a look in the nest. If Mr C isn't in there, we can back out of this room, close the door, maybe barricade it with something, and hope they don't come after us. So I move as fast as I can.

But it turns out they're faster. I make it halfway through my third step before two of them rush me, covering the ground between us in a second, and striking like bowling balls. I fly backwards into the others again, taking out Col and Hallie, and smashing my hip bone hard on the ground.

I bite my lip to stop myself cursing really loud, and try to swallow down the puke that's threatening to force its way upwards. The pain is outrageous.

'You only have yourself to blame,' Gus says, as he helps me up again.

'Did you see how they moved?' Naira says. 'So fast their legs were a blur, and they curled their heads into their bodies before they rammed you. They're definitely the same as the one who took us out before.'

The duck things have returned to their flock and are watching us. The whistling tune keeps playing.

And I don't know how we're going to get to that nest.

'Duckoraptor stand-off,' Gus says.

'Let me check the notebook,' Naira says. 'Maybe there's something that can help.'

And once again we're in a huddle facing a freakish and dangerous enemy, trying to work out what the hell to do next.

'Here's something,' Naira says. 'Due to the increased weight and muscle mass in their legs and torsos, but not their wings, the ducks are unable to fly.'

'So we go high,' Hallie says. 'Follow me.' And she crab-walks to the racks on the right of the door. We follow, carefully, still in our huddle, trying not to set the ducks off, until we're as close to the shelves as we can get without moving closer to the ducks.

'This is gonna be the tricky part,' Hallie says. 'On three. One . . . two . . .'

It's like the ducks can sense we're up to something, because they scurry about, scraping their claws across the ground.

'Three!' Hallie yells, and we all leap for the racks.

The racks are solid metal and screwed into the walls. They look sturdy enough, but who knows if they'll be able to take our weight. I hear a yell from Hallie as I'm pulling myself on to the third shelf, and I turn to see that one of the ducks has her ankle in its beak and is trying to pull her backwards.

'They have freaking teeth!' Hallie shouts.

I look for something to throw, but of course there's nothing. So I pull off my shoe.

But Hallie's a born scrapper. She clings to the racks above her with both hands and she kicks out at the duck with her free foot. The duck's head snaps back and it releases her ankle with an angry hiss.

Naira and Colette reach down to grab Hal's hands, and together they hoist her on to the shelves.

The ducks stand below, making angry noises that are halfway between a quack and a shriek. But they can't follow us up.

The racks creak under our weight, clearly not designed for a group of teenagers to use as a climbing frame.

'Everyone should flatten out,' I say. 'Spread your weight. Then we'll slither to the nest.'

'Of all the antics I thought we'd get up to this evening,' Gus says, as he lies on his belly, 'slithering to a nest didn't make the list.'

The shelves groan with every movement we make. The screws that hold them to the walls seem to loosen bit by bit, and the metal bars begin to rock and tilt slightly. So we go carefully. Knowing we need to hurry, but knowing also that if these racks fall down, we'll be falling down with them, right into a flock of duckoraptors.

It must take us about five minutes to get to the edge of the nest, though it feels like longer. And when we can finally see over the rim, I don't know whether to be frustrated or relieved. No Mr C.

'Where the heck is he then?' Hallie says. 'I'm gonna be so mad with him when we find him.'

'Look at all those eggs, though,' Naira says. 'There must be thirty in there.'

'Thirty duckoraptors to add to the flock. They'll be a big, happy, weird family,' Gus says. 'Look, that one's moving – I think it's going to hatch.'

There's a tapping from inside one of the eggs, which are larger than normal duck eggs – about the size of oranges – and have smooth white shells. The adult ducks must hear the tapping too, because they all climb – with difficulty – back into the nest and gather around it.

'Aw, they want to see their baby being born,' Colette says. 'That's actually dead sweet.'

'Did you not see that one trying to rip my leg off?' Hallie says. 'They are *not* sweet.'

The tappy egg starts rocking around in its trash nest and a large crack splinters down its side. The older ducks nudge at it with their beaks, and pull gently at pieces of shell.

'They're helping their baby break out of the shell,' Gus says. 'Come on, Hal, that's adorable.'

'Literally bit me,' Hallie mutters.

The top of the egg pops off like a lid, and a tiny, mostly bald (but with pink skin and bits of fluff) head pokes out of the top, chirping loudly as it enjoys its new-found freedom. Then it pushes the rest of the egg on to its side and plops out into the nest, looking around at the parent ducks above it through half-open eyes. The ducks gaze at it like it's the most perfect thing they've ever seen.

'OK, fine,' Hallie says. 'That actually is quite cute.'

And then one of the ducks leans over like it's going to snuggle the baby, picks it up in its strange, toothy beak, and swallows it.

'Holy cow!' Hallie yells.

Colette screams and covers her eyes.

Naira turns her head to the wall.

Gus gags and clutches his mouth.

Nature can be harsh. Animals are forced to do what they have to in order to survive. These creatures have no other food source. I know these things. But it's honestly one of the most horrible things I've ever seen.

'I can't believe it ate its baby,' Colette whispers.

And then we hear a tap, tap, tap coming from inside another egg.

CHAPTER TEN

NOT THIS TIME

'No, no, no. This cannot happen again,' Hallie says. 'I'm not allowing it.'

'What are you suggesting we do?' I say. 'Rescue a duckoraptor chick from its cannibal family?'

'We have to,' Hallie says.

'Hallie's right,' Gus says quietly. 'That's an innocent baby. Couldn't hurt anyone. It doesn't deserve to die.'

'What about the others?' Naira gestures at all the other eggs, sitting innocently in the nest.

'We can't save them all,' Colette says. 'And we don't know when they're going to hatch. But we can save this one.'

'And if we raise it with love, instead of hate . . .' Gus is getting into his flow. 'With snuggles instead of violence. With show tunes and grime instead of creepy old nursery rhymes . . . then we could not only save its life, we could fill that life with joy.'

Naira, Hallie and Col start clapping and Gus wipes a pretend tear from his eye.

'Seriously, though,' he says. 'We'll all hate ourselves if we leave it. Look at those cannibal butt-heads eyeing it up.'

The ducks have run over to the wobbling egg and are watching it with greedy eyes.

'I mean obviously we're gonna save it,' I say. 'But how?'

'I'm the strongest,' Gus says. 'Not sure if I've ever mentioned it, but I've been working out and I can take the strain better than any of you. So dangle me.'

We move as fast as we can while trying not to fall, or break the racking so that we end up plunging into the raptor nest. It's not easy, especially with the high stakes involved adding a heap of pressure. The eggshell is starting to crack.

Me and Colette take the higher shelf, holding Gus's feet, while he uses his arms to slowly edge himself down. Hallie and Naira position themselves on lower shelves to help steady him around his waist area. Then we push him as far out from the racks as we can, and bear his weight as we dangle him lower and lower.

The ducks are suspicious, their eyes flicking from the hatching egg, to Gus above their heads, and back again. He's just out of their reach, but if he's going to have a chance of grabbing the egg, we're going to have to dip him right down into the nest.

'Just do it already,' he shouts up to us. 'Hanging upside down like this is making me dizzy.'

'We've got to time it perfectly or we'll drop you,' Naira says. 'You're hard to hold at this angle.'

'The baby has pecked a hole in the top of the egg,' Gus says. 'If we don't go now, it'll be too late.'

'OK, let's go,' I say, because I can see the chick's beak nosing its way out of the hole. And we all strain forward and down, trying to keep a grip on Gus.

'Stop wriggling, Gustav,' Hallie says, as he jerks about like a worm on a hook. 'Or we're going to drop you.'

'But I'm so close,' he says. 'You'll have to swing me further into the centre.'

'You say that like it's easy,' Colette gasps, trying to keep hold of him with her one usable hand. She's sweating. I'm sweating. But we swing, back and forth, trying to get some momentum going.

I hear a cheeping coming from the half-open egg.

'Next swing I can get it,' Gus says, and we all strain to swing him forward.

It's too much for the screws holding the racks to the walls, and a couple of them shoot out of their holes and into the nest. The shelf Colette and I are lying on tilts, giving Gus the extra swing he needs but sending the three of us crashing down into the nest.

I try to sit myself up without crushing any of the eggs around me, though I think a couple of them might have got squashed in the fall. Colette is on the other side, covered in some kind of goo. The duckoraptors are furious, screeching and hissing, and I brace myself for the inevitable blow as one or more of them pounds into me.

'Get ready to run,' Gus yells over the noise. And I don't know what his plan is, but I stand up, reaching a hand over to Col to pull her up too. And then I see Gus throw an egg over the edge of the nest to the back of the room. The duckoraptors shriek and flap their useless wings and fall over each other trying to climb out of the nest to chase after it.

'Go, go, go!' Gus yells. And we scramble out of the nest and head for the door as Hallie and Naira jump off the racks and join us. We get out the door and pull it shut, just as the raptors start charging towards us.

There's a thump in the door a split second later, followed by two more, leaving three dents in the surface. We drag one of the lab counters across the tiled floor to use as a barricade, but the raptors are coming thick and fast, and the door is starting to buckle.

We run out of the lab and close the green door, hoping it will buy us a few more minutes, but it's only a matter of time before the duckoraptors break through and come after us.

'Which way?' Hallie asks.

'We need to go in that direction.' I point. 'It will take us back towards the original lab and the spider tunnels. It's the only place we haven't been, so if Mr C's down here then that's where we'll find him.'

'It also leads towards the well, right?' Naira is sprinting beside me, as the smash and crack of the duckoraptors breaking through the doors rings out behind us.

'Yeah,' I say, trying to match her pace. 'It's our best chance of getting out of here.'

So we run straight ahead, follow the corridor around a right turn and then straight again. As we move, the corridor becomes rougher – the tiled floor replaced by bare stone, the painted walls soon charcoal grey and craggy. The neon strip lights above us end, followed by bare light bulbs screwed into wall fittings, and then no lights at all. We use a phone light to guide us down the main tunnel, and soon see openings to other, smaller passages running off in different directions. We've seen these before.

'Spider burrows,' Naira says, and though she doesn't slow her pace, I can see her shudder. It's hard not to flinch when the shadows seem to shift or pebbles drop.

The spiders we fought all those months ago moved lightning fast and totally silently, alerted to our presence by vibrations in the ground tugging on the strings of their silk. If they were lurking in there now, we'd never know until it was too late.

'We must be under the school field,' I gasp. 'We're almost there.'

'I take back the spider FOMO thing,' Colette says. 'Now that I'm here, I really don't want to see one. You destroyed them all, right?'

'Well . . .' I say. 'Probably.'

'What do you mean "probably"?'

'Did we start a fire down there? Yes,' Hallie says. 'Did we follow it up with a bad-ass explosion? Also yes . . .'

'But some of them could have escaped out of the back of the nest,' Naira says. 'And it seems even more of a possibility now that we know there were more labs and tunnels back here.'

A distant but definite quack-slash-shriek breaks through our spider reminiscing, reminding us that we have more than spiders to worry about.

'They're coming,' Naira gasps, and we speed up as much as we can. It doesn't help that it's dark, or that we're all hurt, or that school shoes are literally the worst footwear for running in. But I know we can't be far now.

And then I hear an unexpected sound from somewhere on our left. I slow a little. Strain my ears. Hoping it will come again so I can work out what it is.

'You heard it too?' Naira says, coming to a stop.

'I heard something.' I stop next to her. 'Not sure what, though.'

The others stop too, and Gus shines the torch around us, three hundred and sixty degrees, so we can see if something's coming.

'It was a whistle,' Naira says. And the rest of us swear, because we instantly think of Mr Latchitt.

'No, not a Latchitt whistle,' Naira says, peering into an opening that looks like it leads to a side tunnel. 'A sports whistle.'

'Mr C,' Colette gasps. 'It has to be.'

The whistle blasts again, shrill and clear. It's coming from the tunnel on our right.

'Detour?' Gus grins, and we don't even need to discuss it. We turn right and plunge into the darkness of the spider burrow.

CHAPTER ELEVEN

GHOSTS

The walls are close around us as we feel our way down the tunnel towards the sound of the whistle. I fight back the feeling of claustrophobia that crowds in with the shadows because I know if I allow it any breathing space, it will grow until it overwhelms me. So I focus on putting one foot in front of the other, and the flicker of hope that's building as the whistle gets louder.

The tunnel twists and turns. In places it's so tight that we graze our elbows as we squeeze our way through. But after a couple of minutes it widens enough that we can run again. So we do. We run. Naira at the front, Hal just behind her. Then me and Colette, then Gus. The path is sloping downwards, and we pick up speed without trying so that we're almost out of control by the time we reach the cavern.

Naira screams and slams into something blocking our way, dropping her phone in the collision. It lands face down, extinguishing our only source of light. I expect to hear the crunch of person into wall, but it doesn't come. I barely make out Hallie ahead of me, trying to stop herself from crashing into the same object, but she hits it hard, right next to where Naira did. And again the only sound is of her screaming.

'Nai, Hal – are you OK?' Colette yells, as we do everything we can to slow ourselves down so that we won't meet the same fate. I skid, and stumble, and my feet fly out from under me so that I drift on my knees for the last part. I land close to the muffled glow of Naira's phone, so I grab it and hold it up, illuminating the cavern.

'You have got to be freaking kidding me,' Gus says behind me.

In front of us is a web. The biggest freaking spiderweb I've ever seen, stretching from floor to ceiling and almost the entire width of the cavern. It must be four or five metres in diameter. Naira and Hallie are stuck in its bone-white strands, trapped next to the fresh corpse of a duckoraptor – probably the one from earlier. Nai and Hal are panicking, desperately trying to detach themselves.

Because lining the shadowed walls either side are the hulking shapes of giant spiders. A whole pack of them – maybe twenty or so. They vary in size, but the smallest ones are at least as big as basketballs, and the largest ones the size of the Finches Heath town bonfire that gets lit every year on 5th November. They're crouched in that position spiders take just as they're about to pounce. And I can see the glint of hundreds of black eyes as the torchlight bounces around the cave.

I swear my heart fully stops for a moment.

We can't beat them. Twenty spiders, only five of us, or three if you count the people who aren't stuck in a web. No weapons.

What do we do?

And then, from a shadowy patch just below the roof of the cavern comes an unmistakeable whistle. I risk flicking my gaze away from the spider army and on to the web. Nai and Hal have stopped struggling and are looking up into the darkness, so I angle the torch to illuminate the spot they're peering at. The light shines on a human-shaped cocoon of spider silk, open at the ends to reveal a pair of shiny shoes and a familiar face. It's Mr C.

I allow myself a second of relief before turning back to the spiders who are still waiting, and watching.

'Why aren't they attacking us?' Naira says. 'It's weird.'

'Maybe they're trying to build the suspense,' Gus

whispers. 'Got to respect their commitment to being terrifying.'

I focus the torchlight on the spider closest to us – a dark brown bristly-haired specimen the size of a truck tyre. It holds its ground, not even flinching when the glare from the phone shines right in its eyes.

'Nah,' I say, taking a step closer to it. 'Nai's right – something's up.'

'Angelo . . .' Colette says. 'Please don't do what I think you're going to do.'

I keep my eyes on the spider, watching for any flicker of movement. Nothing. It could be playing dead to lure us in. It might be waiting for the perfect moment to attack. But the Latchitt spiders are smart. They'd know that they massively outnumber us, and I don't think they'd waste their time in a drawn-out ambush.

'He wouldn't,' Hallie gasps from the web. 'Don't do it, Angelo.'

'It's the only way we'll know for sure,' I say, taking another step towards the spider. Still no movement. So I lunge forward, covering the space between us in just a second or two. I'm sweating, half expecting to be caught in its mandibles. But it doesn't move. I swipe at one of its legs with the phone because even though I'm good with spiders generally, I don't feel OK enough to want to feel the prickle of its thick hairs with my skin.

There's a crack as the leg snaps off and falls to the ground in a crumbly heap. Motes of crusty spider dust rise up into the air around me.

'Is it dead?' Gus says.

'It's not an actual spider,' I say, looking at the remains of the spider more closely. 'It's an exoskeleton. Spiders shed their bodies as they outgrow them.'

'So it's just a spider shell?' Gus says.

'Kind of.' I nudge one of the other legs with the toe of my shoe. It disintegrates like ash.

'Thank god,' Colette says, rushing forward to the web. 'Mr C? Are you conscious?'

Mr Canton has dried blood covering one side of his face. His hair is all over the shop. The shiny shoes that we know he saves for special occasions are scuffed and caked in dirt. But he's alive. And we know this because every few seconds he blows on the whistle that's hanging out of his mouth, making him look like a retired cowboy, sitting on a porch swing, sucking on a pipe.

Instead of answering in normal human words, he starts humming.

'What's that?' Hallie is pulling against the web like it might suddenly ping off her. 'A nursery rhyme?'

'It's the *Spider-Man* theme,' Colette says, jogging

over to her to try to help. 'Anyone got anything sharp? I don't think we can snap this by pulling – it's too stretchy. We need to cut it.'

'And how the heck are we supposed to get Mr Canton down?' Gus walks to the web and carefully pokes it with his finger. His finger sticks like the web is coated in superglue. 'Oh,' he says. 'Now I'm stuck too.'

'Well, why did you touch it?' Hallie yells. 'Did you think me and Naira were faking?'

'Calm down, Hal,' Naira says. 'The more we move, the worse we're making it for ourselves. We need to think this through.'

'Oh man, my shoe's stuck now,' Gus says.

'Did you touch the web with your shoe, Gustav?' Naira says.

'It was an accident,' he says. And then, 'Maybe,' under his breath.

'Don't touch the web with any other body parts,' Naira says with a sigh.

Mr Canton has gone quiet, so I shine the torch right in his face. It feels mean but we need him to stay awake so we can get out of here. If we find a way to get everyone unstuck from the web. He opens his eyes super wide, and starts humming 'Spider-Man' again, but in a way like he's distracted by something. Sometimes when I'm talking to one of the popular kids at school because I have to, for a group project or something, and I know they wish they weren't paired with me, I can see their eyes shift away from my face and start looking over my shoulder for someone more interesting. And that's what Mr C looks like he's doing right now. So I turn around, but all I see are the exoskeletons.

'I think I know how we can cut it,' I say, running back to the spider skins for a better look. 'If we can find a fresher skeleton that doesn't collapse, we can pull off its mandibles and use those to saw the threads.'

'By your logic, the biggest one has to be the freshest, right?' Naira says.

'Which would be that donny in the corner,' Gus says.

I look into the shadowiest corner of the cavern where Gus is pointing with his unstuck hand. He's right – the exoskeleton lurking there is colossal, with mandibles as long as my arms and five times as thick. If anything's going to cut through the web, it's those.

I squeeze around the smaller spider skins, sweeping this fresh exoskeleton with the torchlight. It does look newer than the others. Glossier. Less dusty.

I move the phone to my right hand so my left is free to yank the mandible – it looks like it will be harder to wrench off than the leg on the first exoskeleton.

Behind me, Mr C is manically humming the *Spider-Man* theme, the sound of it echoing around the dome of the cave. I have a second of thinking how surreal this situation is. Like, the absolute insanity of it all. And then I grab the mandible about halfway up so I don't get cut on the serrated part, and I pull.

It pulls back.

I scream and let go, as the mammoth spider, which is very much alive, scuttles forward.

I back away, knowing I'm backing towards a potentially indestructible web, but physically unable to not put whatever distance I can between myself and the monster in front of me.

There's a moment of shocked silence as the others also take in what we're facing. I glance at the four of them over my shoulder, and it's like how I imagine the reaction would be if the Death Star appeared above the earth and fired up its primary weapon. Too shocked to scream. Inevitable horror incoming.

This spider is like nothing we've seen before. Its head and abdomen are bulbous but elongated, so its body is much longer and more powerful than the ones we fought before. And as it unfurls itself from the crouch, I can see that its legs are something else – twice as long as I would have expected, so that its knees are higher than my head. The colour is strange too – an off-white, slightly translucent, like yellowed teeth.

'OK, so we've found the one monster I'd rather fight in the dark,' Hallie whispers.

I force myself to calm, look it right in the eyes. Because nothing bad ever goes away if you just ignore it. And I need to try to get my head around it.

First thought: giant spider.

Second thought: run or fight?

Third thought: school motto – Dread Wood High, fight or die.

CHAPTER TWELVE

UNLIKELY ALLIES

'Col, grab an actual dead mandible and cut the others free,' I say, trying to keep the spider's attention on me, because it's the only chance I can see for us to get out of here. Small as it is.

I rip a mandible off a nearby skeleton to use as a weapon. It's brittle and half the size of the living mandibles clacking just a metre or so from my head, but it's the best I can do because what else is there in this freaking horrible cave? I thrust it forward, aiming for the spider's football-sized eyes. At least they're easy to aim for. The spider dodges, springing to the right, away from my pathetic excuse for a weapon, and then pulls back on its spider knees like it's going for a full attack.

I can hear the yells of the others behind me, and I hope Col's cutting those threads away. Getting everyone free. They could still escape, even if I don't. I try to swallow, my throat dry and swollen and feeling like it might close up completely, leaving me to gasp for breath. My mind races through my options: dodge left, dodge right, duck and roll? My life will depend on whatever choice I make next.

Then I hear the scuffle of many feet back in the tunnel we just squeezed through, and my heart thuds. The duckoraptors are here. They cannonball into the cave, some of them crashing straight into the web, the others pulling back and looking around, hissing angrily. The spider hesitates. Turns to face the new enemy. Or prey maybe. Either way, it works for us.

I run.

Naira is already free and working on Mr C with a mandible. Colette is cutting the last strands away from Hallie.

'Help Nai,' I gasp. 'I'll get Gus.'

I dart over to where Gus stands frozen in fear – his finger, shoe and for some reason his ear all glued to the sticky strings. I attack the threads of the web with the urgency of someone who has only seconds before he and his friends are devoured by a creature that looks like it teleported here from prehistoric times.

'What's happening?' I say, not wanting to turn away from the web.

'Just your classic mutant spider versus duckoraptor battle,' he says. 'The duckoraptors have the numbers, obvs, and they're cannonballing the spider's legs which is a smart move.'

The strands sticking his leg to the web give way.

'If you'd have asked me who'd win this, I would have said Big Donny, no probs,' Gus says. 'But it's actually close. Donny keeps stumbling. If the duckoraptors can break the legs they could take him.'

I can smell biscuits on his breath as I cut the web from his ear.

'Oof, Donny just impaled a raptor with one of his mandem things. Raptor's just hanging there while the others go full-in on Donny.'

'Almost there,' I say, moving to Gus's hand.

'I wouldn't wanna call it, you know?' Gus says.

'Lucky for us,' I say, stepping back from the web. 'You're done.'

'I'm free,' Gus says, staring at his formerly stuck finger like it's the most amazing thing he's seen in his life.

Hallie, Naira and Colette finish cutting the strings around Mr C, and he drops to the floor in a heap. Then we hoist him upright, not even waiting to work out what injuries he has. We have to get out of this cave.

'We need you to walk, Mr C,' Hallie says. 'Or we're not going to make it.'

Mr C makes a visible effort to hold himself up,

to firm up his legs and raise his head.

'Well done, sir,' Col says. 'Now which way do we go?'

Naira's been using her torch to look into every corner of the cavern. 'There's a small tunnel to the right there, just behind the web. Let's go.' And she leads us through the gap into the darkness beyond.

We don't hesitate – whatever lies beyond the cavern can't be any worse than what we're dealing with right here, right now. So we run. Expecting every second for either the duckoraptors or the spider to catch up with us.

Mr C stumbles along at first but gets steadier on his feet as we go, until he's managing on his own. None of us talk. We just run for our lives. The passage is sloping down again, and for a minute I'm worried that we're just going deeper and deeper underground, but then I see a dead end ahead.

'It's the well,' Hallie gasps.

And the light from the phone shows that she's right. It's the bottom of a circular, human-made hole that stretches vertically upwards. The sides are lined with neatly cut stones, dislodged in places by tree roots growing into the gaps between them. I might even be able to climb up using the twisted roots as hand and footholds. But I don't need to. The beam from Naira's phone glints on something metallic attached to the left side. A ladder.

I put my foot on the bottom rung and yank the sides hard with my hands, testing its strength. It doesn't move even a tiny bit. I climb up five rungs, ignoring the sting from my cut-up hands, the burn in my muscles and the throbbing in my knees. The ladder is solid.

'Can it take our weight, Angelo?' Naira says from below me.

I look down and grin. 'Let's get out of here.'

*

When we get back to student services, there's a note scribbled on A4 paper and Sellotaped to the door.

Subjects talks overran. Choccie Chat cancelled.

Mr C rips it from the door, scrunches it up with a sigh and stuffs it in his pocket. Then he pushes the door and holds it open for us as we file in and collapse on the sofas.

'I know you're disappointed, sir,' Naira says. 'But it was probably for the best. I mean, look at the state of us.'

The parts of our school uniforms that haven't been ripped off and used as bandages are bloodstained, filthy and torn. We're cut, bruised, swollen and sticky, with patches of unidentifiable goo in random places.

'Nai-Nai's right,' Gus says. 'You guys have literally never looked more wrecked. I mean, I make it work, but the rest of you are a disgrace.' Then he jumps us with way more enthusiasm and energy than he should have at this point in the evening, and skips over to the vending machine. 'Shall I do the honours?' He starts tapping the buttons without waiting for an answer. 'Hot choccies for everyone.'

'Question for you, Gustav . . .' Mr C says.

'If it's about my sick dinner lady hat, then I'm happy to tell you there are more hanging up in the kitchen. Though I'm not sure you can rock it like I can.'

'That's not what I was going to –' Mr C says.

'How did you end up under the kitchen, sir?' I ask. 'We came looking for you . . .'

'After the specified fifteen minutes-ish,' Hallie says.

'And you were gone.' I take my cup of hot choccie from Gus.

'We found your clipboard by the trapdoor,' Colette says. 'And ink from your pen.'

'Well – and don't think you can distract me away from my question forever, by the way – I was in the kitchen preparing the refreshment trolley, and I heard what sounded like a baby crying. So I followed the sound and discovered a grate in the pantry floor that was askew. When I lifted the grate and saw the ladder, I thought I'd better take a look. But I didn't factor in my fancy event footwear – these shoes are not very grippy . . .' He points at his now bashed-up posh shoes. 'I slipped, I think. Hit my head. And everything that happened from then is a bit of a blur. Oh god, was there a baby down there? We have to go back!' He starts to get up from the sofa.

'There wasn't a baby,' Colette says. 'Not the human kind anyway.'

'Thank god.' He sinks back on to the sofa.

'Just freaky bushbabies,' Hallie says.

'Aw, bushbabies,' Mr C says. 'Aren't they supposed to be cute?'

'No!' we all shout.

Gus hands Mr C a hot choccie and pats him on the shoulder. 'This should settle you down a bit, Mr C.'

Mr C takes a sip and smiles. 'Now back to my question, Gustav . . . What in the blazes is moving around in your pocket?'

I look over at Gus to see there *is* something in his pocket. It forms a ball shape under the fabric of his blazer and is softly chirping.

Gus puts his hand in gently and pulls out the weirdest duckling the world has ever seen – a mix of scales and fluff, with its blackcurrant eyes half open and gazing up at Gus's face.

'What the bejesus is that?' Mr Canton almost spills his hot chocolate.

'This is Egg,' Gus says. 'And I'm his new mama.'

'Do I want to know where Egg came from and how he happens to be in your possession?' Mr C says.

Gus shakes his head. 'Probably not, sir.'

'Right then,' Mr C says. 'Well, at least we managed to recruit one new member to Dread Wood High this evening.'

'And when he gets bigger he's going to be a kick-ass fighter,' Hallie says.

'Maybe he can help us battle our next Latchitt monster,' Naira says, stroking Egg under his fluffy chin. 'Because I'm sure there will be more of those in future.'

'In addition to the ones still lurking in the basement,' I say. 'Someone's going to have to deal with them at some point. We could do with some back-up.'

'Cheers to Egg.' Colette raises her paper cup.

'Cheers to Egg,' we all say, air-clinking our hot choccies.

I lean over and tickle the baby's head. 'Welcome to Club Loser.'

HAPPY WORLD BOOK DAY!

Choosing to read in your spare time can make you happier and more successful. We want that for every young person.

NOW YOU'VE READ THIS BOOK YOU COULD:

• Swap it • Read it again • Recommend it to a friend • Talk about it

WHERE WILL YOUR READING JOURNEY TAKE YOU NEXT?

Why not challenge a friend, teacher, local bookseller or librarian to recommend your next read based on your interests?

 Find your **LOCAL LIBRARY**

Find your **NEAREST BOOKSELLER**

START A BOOK RECOMMENDATION CHAT!

• I really liked... (What should I read next?)
• I like books that have... (character types, plot types)
• I would like to try... (genre or non-fiction or poetry)
...can you recommend a good place to start?
• I am interested in...

WORLD
BOOK
DAY™

Even when the pressure is on, choosing to read

# BOOSTS YOUR
>>> WELLBEING <<<

Make a **READING HABIT** - try scheduling 10 minutes a day

Choose your **READING** to match your **MOOD**

Hide distractions to find **YOUR FOCUS**

GET READY - take a breath or two

MIX IT UP - try an audiobook on a walk

SOCIALISE - chat about it, read together or join a book club

DISCOVER your next read at **WORLDBOOKDAY.COM**

CHECK OUT THE REST OF THE DREAD WOOD SERIES!

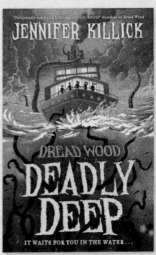

DON'T MISS THE LATEST ADVENTURE!

A COLLECTION OF 13 SPINE-TINGLING TALES!

JENNIFER KILLICK

Jennifer Killick is the author of the Dread Wood series, *Crater Lake, Crater Lake, Evolution* and the Alex Sparrow series. Jennifer regularly visits schools and festivals, and her books have been selected four times for the Reading Agency's Summer Reading Challenge. She lives in Uxbridge, in a house full of children, animals and books. When she isn't busy mothering (which isn't often) she loves to watch scary movies and run as fast as she can, so she is fully prepared for witches, demons, and the zombie apocalypse.